# This Morning Sam Went to Mars

## A book about paying attention

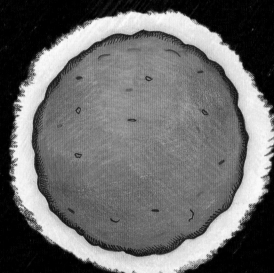

Nancy Carlson

**Library of Congress Cataloging-in-Publication Data**
Carlson, Nancy L., author, illustrator.
 This morning Sam went to Mars : a book about paying attention  / Nancy Carlson.
    pages cm
 Summary: "Eight-year-old Sam has a powerful brain but needs some help focusing. The doctor gives Sam lots of strategies to try, like staying organized, eating better food, and asking for help when he needs it. Sam's favorite strategy? Make time for imagination"— Provided by publisher.
 ISBN-13: 978-1-57542-433-0 (hardcover)
 ISBN-10: 1-57542-433-9 (hardcover)
 ISBN-13: 978-1-57542-434-7 (pbk.)
 [1. Attention—Fiction. 2. Imagination—Fiction.]  I. Title.
 PZ7.C21665Tk 2013
 [E]—dc23
                                        2012046485

eBook ISBN: 978-1-57542-638-9

Reading Level Grade 2; Interest Level Ages 4–8;
Fountas & Pinnell Guided Reading Level K

Edited by Eric Braun
Cover and interior design by Tasha Kenyon

10 9 8 7 6 5 4 3 2 1
Printed in Hong Kong
P17200213

**Free Spirit Publishing Inc.**
Minneapolis, MN
(612) 338-2068
help4kids@freespirit.com
www.freespirit.com

**Free Spirit offers competitive pricing.**
Contact edsales@freespirit.com for pricing information on
multiple quantity purchases.

To my pal, Talla. Thank you for all your support this year!

This morning, Sam went to Mars.

1

When he got back, he was late for school again.
He had to quickly . . .

POP!

finish breakfast

get dressed

and find his homework.

2

He missed the bus,
and his dad said,
"Sam, you need to focus!"

3

When Sam finally got to school, he went on a deep sea adventure.

When he got back, he had missed six words on his spelling test.
His teacher said, "Sam, you need to focus!"

People were always telling Sam to focus. When they did, he felt . . .

frustrated

sad

and dumb.

Sam's dad knew he wasn't dumb, so he brought him to a doctor.

8

Sam told the doctor about people always saying, "Focus, Sam!"

Sam also talked about the stories he writes and the pictures he paints.
And he told her about his cool ideas for inventions and adventures.

The doctor said, "Wow, Sam, you are lucky! You have a very powerful brain. With that brain, you can do great things in your life."

"To make the most of that powerful brain, you need to take care of it," she said.

"How do I do that?" Sam asked. He liked the idea of having a powerful brain.

"Oh, I have lots of good ideas," the doctor said. "Cutting way down on junk food is a good place to start."

"Oh, man."

"Don't worry, Sam. There are lots of people to help you," the doctor said. "Your parents can help by keeping yummy, healthy snacks at home."

"Super foods like blueberries are *extra* healthy."

"You can help, too. Lay out your clothes before bed."

"And learn how to organize your homework."

"Be sure to get a good night's sleep. Sleep is good for your brain."

"At school, clean up your desk, and ask if you can move it away from the window."

"Ask your teacher for help when you need it."

POP!

REA FUN

"You can even ask a friend to help you remember to pay attention."

"And be sure to find time to use your imagination. It's awesome!"

15

Sam worked hard to follow the doctor's suggestions.

He ate super foods every day.

He tried to stay organized at home . . .

. . . and at school.

He asked his teacher for help.

Sam tried hard to pay attention, but . . .

. . . he still heard people tell him to focus.

And then one day . . .

. . . Sam got to school on time
with his homework!

And he got most of his
spelling words right.

He also wrote a really great story that day.

Sam kept trying hard.

Soon he noticed that he hadn't heard anyone say, "Focus, Sam!" in a while.

These days Sam is not perfect, but he pays attention most of the time. And he always makes sure he has time . . .

. . . to go to Mars.

# Note to Parents and Teachers: Helping Kids with Attention Challenges

Many young children, like Sam, have trouble paying attention sometimes—or a lot of the time! They may be distractible, impulsive, or hyperactive. For most of these kids, the difficulty focusing comes at school or at other times when they are expected to pay attention to things that may be hard or boring for them. The same kid who can't concentrate for 10 minutes on a math problem can often spend hours reading a book about knights, playing capture the flag with friends, or writing a story about Mars.

Whether the kids in your life are very distractible, like Sam, or could maybe just use a *little* nudge in the focus department, it's important to keep things positive. The following guidelines can help nurture these characteristics while also improving kids' focus in all areas.

- **Make sure they get enough sleep.** Most kids between the ages of 5 and 9 need 10 to 11 hours of sleep a night. Sleep improves focus and helps the brain stay healthy. To help kids get enough sleep, have them go to bed and get up at the same time every day, even on weekends.

- **Help them eat a healthy diet.** Junk foods like sweets and salty snacks are not only unhealthy for the body, they're also unhelpful for the brain. It's okay to have junk food treats every now and then, but keep them to a minimum. Healthy foods like fruits and vegetables are good for the body and brain. Some foods called super foods are especially good because they have lots of vitamins, minerals, protein, and good fats and oils. These include nuts like almonds and walnuts, seeds like pumpkin and sunflower seeds, oily fish like salmon and tuna, broccoli, blueberries, spinach, carrots, tomatoes, wheat, eggs, and milk (to name only a few). Encourage kids to drink plenty of water, too. These foods and drinks help kids feel great and help their brains run efficiently.

- **Provide structure.** Kids work best when they have predictable routines and a place to store important materials in school and at home. If possible, provide physical space at home for their homework and an unchanging place to do it.

- **Reduce distractions.** Move students with wandering eyes away from the window or door and closer to the front of the class. Clutter is a distraction, too, so help kids keep desks, lockers, and bedrooms clean and organized.

- **Make time for physical activity.** Even a short break for exercise can help refresh the brain.

- **Encourage creativity.** "Distractible" often goes hand-in-hand with "creative." Encourage creativity (at appropriate times). It makes kids happy and it's good exercise for the brain.

Most children with attention challenges are curious, creative, and energetic—positive qualities that will help them be happy and successful in life. Nurturing their creativity while helping tame their attention challenges is the best way to provide support.

# About the Author and Illustrator

Nancy Carlson is an accomplished children's book author and illustrator who has published more than 60 books. A lifelong Minnesotan, Nancy graduated from the Minneapolis College of Art and Design with a major in printmaking. She believes that life should be fun for everyone, but especially for children. This optimistic message permeates her picture books and provides a positive counterpoint to much of what children are influenced by in today's society. Her characters aren't always perfect. They often have fears, anxieties, and learning differences. Through her books, kids learn to cope with a range of challenges. They can learn that they don't have to be perfect to be good people. Her characters also convey positive messages without being "preachy." They gently remind children what is right.

Nancy is also a guest author and illustrator at over 150 school classrooms each year, and has touched the lives of thousands of children across the United States. She lives in Minneapolis. Learn more about Nancy and her books—and check out her daily doodles—at her website, **www.nancycarlson.com.**

# More Great Books from Free Spirit

## ParentSmart/KidHappy™ Series

*by Stacey R. Kaye, MMR, illustrated by Elizabeth O. Dulemba*

Children will love the full-color pictures and tender stories, and parents and caregivers will learn the language of positive parenting. With honesty and gentle humor, each book shows parents how to handle daily transitions by giving encouragement, offering choices, and validating feelings. The result: you get through everyday challenges with less stress while building your child's emotional intelligence. *32 pp., illust., 4-color, H/C, 8¼" x 8¼". Ages 3–6.*

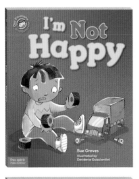

## Our Emotions and Behavior Series

*by Sue Graves, illustrated by Desideria Guicciardini*

Small children have big feelings. The Our Emotions and Behavior series uses cheerful, brightly illustrated stories to help kids understand how their emotions and actions are related—and how they can learn to manage both. Follow along as Noah, Ben, Nora, and their friends discover ways to deal with fears, sadness, rules, and sharing. At the end of each book, a two-page series of pictures invites kids to tell a story in their own words. A special section for adults suggests discussion questions and ideas for guiding children to talk about their feelings. *32 pp., illust., 4-color, H/C, 7¾" x 9½". Ages 4–8.*

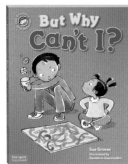

## Zach Rules Series

*by William Mulcahy, illustrated by Darren McKee*

Zach, his brothers Alex and Scott, and his parents are a typical family. The boys struggle with getting along, frustrations, social issues, and other everyday problems typical with kids ages 5 to 8. Each book in the Zach Rules series presents a single, simple storyline involving one such problem. As each story develops, Zach and readers learn straightforward tools for coping with their struggles. The tools are presented graphically to make them easier to understand and remember. Each book concludes with a short note to adults to help parents, teachers, counselors, and other grown-ups reinforce the books' messages and practice the skills with their kids. *32 pp., illust., 4-color, H/C, 8" x 8". Ages 5–8.*

---

**Interested in purchasing multiple quantities and receiving volume discounts?**
Contact edsales@freespirit.com or call 1.800.735.7323 and ask for Education Sales.

**Many Free Spirit authors are available for speaking engagements, workshops, and keynotes.**
Contact speakers@freespirit.com or call 1.800.735.7323.

---

*For pricing information, to place an order, or to request a free catalog, contact:*

# free spirit PUBLISHING®

**217 Fifth Avenue North • Suite 200 • Minneapolis, MN 55401-1299**
**toll-free 800.735.7323 • local 612.338.2068 • fax 612.337.5050**
**help4kids@freespirit.com • www.freespirit.com**